EVERYTHING TO DO WITH YOU

stories by

SEAN TAYLOR

Published by SEVEN7H TANGENT in San Francisco, CA

Edited by Laura Chapman and Lauren Taylor.

Book design by Sean Taylor & J. Brandon Loberg

Cover art copyright 2010 Joesph Mauk

Titles in Didot- Set in Palatino

Second Edition

"His Stop" previously appeared in the 16th and Mission Review

ISBN-13: 978-0-6924-6632-2

ISBN-10: 069-2-4663-20

In the elevator before the earthquake,

in the river after the flood,

before I met you, at first we smirked.

*For Charlie Getter, Brandon Loberg
and everyone at 16th and Mission*

Also by Sean Taylor
Your Smallest Bones (2015)

Contents

Why won't you lie?

Small talk is when you lost your job, when your grandmother's wedding ring was going, going, gone down the garbage disposal.

I was halfway home when I realized it was raining, and after five drops I realized I had forgotten my umbrella at work. Good, I thought, I can sport that sopping-puppy look, and when I get in she'll sit me in front of that shoddy old heater of ours, remove my damp socks and rub my cold feet. I'll wear this as if I have just returned from a jaunty mountain expedition-placed a flag upon our new kingdom, and all I have to do was walk home from work in the rain. Of course she isn't home when I get in, and the apartment is cold as ever. The microclimates of an in-law in San Francisco can be embarrassing, much more evidently so when the wind wanders the entirety of your square footage. So I headed out to crank up the landlords water heater, the dial being my favorite bidding war with the old Irish women, and at level eight it knocks like an old rocket about to take off, level seven just sounds like the warmth wants out.

So I am faced with two options in hopes of conveying the idea I've only just arrived and very much need warmth. Option one is stand by the door and when I hear her key, snap on the lights as she enters. Option two is have a beer and get the couch wet. Option two sounds like an unwanted-dog option. Option one sounds like something you should never tell someone about. I am not an unwanted dog nor am I something you should never tell someone about.

She works downtown and usually taxis home, the sole purpose of this is so she can open a bottle of Syrah that she will need me to help her finish, keeping me from my beers. If I beat her home, I have my beer and she will save the wine for another night and turn to the vodka. I will be wine free.

Any other day I would be celebrating, but not today. Today I want to come home to her like our apartment is a house and like our problems are waiting for the bathwater to warm up and feeding the dog we don't have.

I am the dog we don't have.

As I linger in the hallway I notice I'm dripping evidence, dripping like an hourglass of proof of my existence, and I can hear the drops, like a ticking clock.

I run, run like you do when the trash bag breaks and drips all that gross trash juice, I run into the bathroom and grab the blow dryer and start to blow dry my existence from the scene of the crime err, lie. Maybe a vacuum would do better; the cord is always two inches too short or not at all. One hundred percent of crimes make a mess. Do vacuums suck up moisture and lies?

I can hear steps, quick street steps, nice lady shoe steps and then as I am diagnosing these to be hers, I hear the key grind and turn.

She floods into the door, soaked head to toe, worse then I ever was, and stares down at me. I'm in my grace half shivering, with a beer, blow-drying the first steps of the hallway.

My dignity folds like a dying star.

She's cold and confused, her mascara is running down her cheeks like she's been crying and for this I love her more.

"What the fuck?"

"I didn't want to get the carpet wet?"

"You're lying, try again."

"I like your blow dryer?"

"That's just weird. Again?"

I think we should move on, away from this moment, but the hallway is very narrow and I am entirely a fire hazard. I am a sopping wet excuse-less fire hazard.

I Clear my throat...

Remember in August when we met? Your father had just passed and you held yourself hostage on a rowboat in the middle of Stow Lake. It began to rain so hard, and your boat started to fill up with pounds of the bay. They sent me out like a suicide negotiator in a kayak to save you. Remember I had only just started that job that week and was granted to do so thanks to my falsified Certified CPR card and a copy of *Sailing for Dummies*? Remember when your mascara was running but you kept saying you weren't crying, that it was the weather that had you trapped?

"I'm telling you the weather has me trapped."

"And?"

And out on that lake that day you yelled "desperation please!"

And I heard "desperate pleas?"

I wondered about first impressions.

"And I love you? And thought we should get home at the same time so nobody is predominately responsible for warming up the covers, cause you know, I know you're just better at warming up the covers."

In August when we met I told you to get into my kayak, that when your ship sinks the preservation acid in the lake will bleed your socks and dye your feet in argyle designs.

And you said, "I like you more when you lie."

And I asked you if the lotion you wore on your legs contained Lanolin, as the scent does attract Koi fish, and whether you felt any nibbling.

"You're as curious as my toes."

And then you threw your phone into the lake, then your purse.

So I told you to let go.

Then you threw yourself.

And the toes of your cheap socks broke apart in the Koi fishes' throats and I got fired for diving in after you and not the sinking rowboat.

By the time we reached the shore the ducks all mocked us half dry like showboats, you told me I was bleeding from the head and I said good, now you know me better.

In the hallway I stood up and pushed her drippy bangs behind her ear and kissed the part of her cheek finger painted by gravity with mascara and rainwater. When I draw back she's smiling and impatient.

And she looked at our feet and proclaimed, "What a wonderful puddle we always find ourselves in."

And we don't talk about the weather.

"Oh, and, my socks are wet" she says for the second time this year.

Everything to do with You

I used to know this character, he would tell me stories all day. No, they weren't stories. He said they were currencies or profiles or hopes.

They were really just people.

He, himself, wandered in pockets alone, slept only in trench coat robes and his eyes were always moving up and down like a Japanese typewriter that doesn't exist. Upon the question of his name, well, he would squint real hard and say something to the effect of… "Charles? Or Charels?" It was almost as if he cared less for himself than anyone else.

Still he said, "There was this couple last night on Gough and Pine that longed for blinds in night time windows, that tortured the fireflies with screens and screams, tortured their neighbors with fake exciting things, like fire drills and de-railed trains on loud TV screens and perpetual fainting scenes."

Like gunfire this one, a real Tommy gun, crop-dusting his memory.

There was a bird with one good wing, it would fly in circles around his loft, lie dizzy on the ottoman on its back, swearing it was going somewhere, but always like a homing pigeon, proud it found its way back.

He even told me about this homeless man that spent most of his time in the airport, on the baggage terminals, that his family were frequent flyers and he was full of hot air hopes. Sure, they never got him off the ground-but he thought, he knew, he thought baggage is always worth picking up.

I don't know, I could go on all day with these little niches he found in every person that made them at least a little interesting.

Everyone collects baseball cards.

I know this one time he told me he rode the train all day, from nine to five, so he could find this old operators' eyes, he promised me that they hid in his cheeks and when he blinked they plummeted to his feet if only for seconds to once again fall asleep beside his Mexican wife on the beach. The man would go without socks and with the most uncomfortable of shoes, if only to prove he needed her to rub his terribly sore feet. He earned every second of her affection and he was the only train driver to work without gloves, telling his co-workers he had only hoped the blisters would last another night for him to procure another set of her delicate crooning kisses.

They were all very short though, and I could never understand that. It seemed as soon as he started one he was out the door looking for another.

I'm pretty sure the shortest one went like this.

This girl the other day, just smiled.

And I told him "and," I asked him "and?"

But that was the first one he ever told me, he said you have to start somewhere, that he told a thousand people "This girl the other day, just smiled"

And he would watch the faces of his listeners and wait for their reactions as if they were telling him a story. I had no stories, I immediately felt foolish, I had a question, and I was waiting for him. How I wanted an answer, to know exactly what he meant. He told me half of the people asked the same question as I, or just walked away. The other half left lit candles in their eyes letting their ideas parachute out like confetti, full of other niches.

They would finish his sentences. "This is what missing you is," they would say when they were finished.

They would tell him about her hips; the way they themselves smile the way belly dancers smile with their hips. Or those cynical girls, you know the ones. With lips small and sure of straight lines that begin with a smirk, lips tight, then to sneer, followed by relief tied ear to ear. That when she really meant it she didn't have anything to do with it-and oh how she hated it. But it was a smile forced upon her face. Then there were the ugly ones, but they never knew it. Those big brassy smiles that pinched tight their eyes as if their faces were over worked contracting orifices of happiness. And it was beautiful and she never saw it. The real ones never come before mirrors and photos, he tells me; well as often as lightning if you get the timing right.

Some days he would swear he was hearing about the same girl, he would put off the old bag woman that haunts the dairy isle, he wouldn't even care about this great hole in one man's cheek, he just wanted to find this girl. And after his listeners were finished finishing his stories they would wipe their eyes and say, "This is what missing you is." Then thank him. He didn't write because he called it therapy, if it was for him or them I'm not sure, probably both.

So he would tell me every other month or so how his great chase was going. He was collecting the same kind of caricatures you find at crime scenes, his listeners were mere witnesses. He narrowed down his descriptions to what any eighteenth-century artist would conclude to be Venus. And I told him there was no girl, no specific girl.

He slammed the door twice that day, once when he came in, then again when he left. About a month later I received a check in the mail for a new door or so I thought. It was two thousand dollars and attached a note read, "Thanks for the title."

A week later I got a phone call from an old friend saying I was mentioned in some new book, linear notes or something said it was called "No Specific Girl." I picked it up the next day and sure enough he had kept all those descriptions of all those smiles, each page dramatically different, but still in love like the last. A lot of people are saying they only read it to find theirs, to read theirs over and over again. I'm pretty sure that's why anybody reads anything, to feel like they are part of it, to feel like somebody's listening even if they have to hear it in print.

And then there were the girls, there were the girls that stood on witness stands like testimonials, they pointed to their supposed page and then waited for their royalties.

The courtroom drawings drew through their best hopes, because they didn't look so smiley on those watercolors and pencil shavings against the great oak countertops of a cold as hell courtroom.

He came over again just last week and told me all this, my friend, my character. He told me none of the trials ever presented any amiable evidence. They were acquitted, like smiles, and then he smirked.

So I asked him one last time and sincerely about the first one, the first girl the other day that just smiled, I asked him if she knew.

He told me in a second, "She didn't know at all, none of the real ones did, it's how I knew I'd win every time in court."

And I said, "How?" I said, "How?"

He told me something he only just learned about everything.

"There are some things one cannot see in the mirror, it's the right angle-I suppose, it's sublime. Nobody can ever see, personally what their lovers see in them. They can't escape their eyes, their angles, and their mind. Art in general alone in a hallway is nothing, it is the critics or the audience or the ones lost in its shades that know it best. Humans are no different. They will never know themselves the same way the people that love them do, they will never understand who they are from their unilateral point of view."

"Sure thing, but who was the first?" I begged.

He told me he once held a mirror to the Mona Lisa, he told me she didn't flinch for a second, she didn't even recognize herself.

His Stop

I woke up on the N Judah today; inbound, on my way to work, with my bowtie in my hand like a chimp in a white tuxedo. Sometime while I was sleeping (and I am assuming the reason for my departure from such a state) a man sat down next to me. This old thin wino, his blood cherry eyes sun burnt beyond pigment staring down at me, his breathing constantly tapping me on the shoulder. It's ten thirty-seven in the morning, and I have made a new friend.

His head isn't balding, I like to think it's selectively growing or perhaps continentally drifting apart, and in the center, the Atlantic Ocean of his head is beat red like lava and I ask myself if I am still awake. His choice of dress is Vietnam fatigues lined with pillowcases and dreams. The man has a bottle of wine from Napa in one hand, half empty-or full, with the cork bobbing in it all friendly in a small swishy sea of wishes. His other hand was firm and ripe with sign language murmurs. Details aside, I try harder to recognize the label than I do to read it, as his shaky hands give me motion sickness. I'm hoping its one of the bottles we sell to rich white people on the higher floors of my workplace, a four star hotel. Nothing comes to mind. I notice instantly the bottle is a two thousand five and I ask the man who mutters and stutters and mumbles to himself if that was a good year. This of course sends him into a mean case of the no's one after the other and I'm sure a nope and a fuck join the negative party in his mouth.

Miscommunication is common when you talk to someone with such a constant drunken disposition so I tell him I was referring to the wine. The man jumps up, it is his stop, where he's going I'm pretty sure the bottle has got him further than this train ever will, it is definitely his stop.

Spilling milk was fun when our parents told us it was just that; spilt milk, however some of us never grew out of this phase.

Upon his departure from the seat and while putting on his jacket, multi-tasked this one, his arm swings back and (I want to say gently because I was there and it might hold up in court) gently brushes the behind of an Asian woman. No, she wasn't a woman, she was a girl in her mothers clothing. She gives off that inborn high-pitched squeal selected since the birth of time so as to gesture something has caught my backside by surprise, the world is now over. And she gives it; the noise alone is terrible, if you're drunk and crazy it will knock you off your feet.

And so my friend is off his feet and on the floor, down fast like spilt milk during an air raid. He rolls over from his back into a forest of legs clad in trunks of shiny shoes, and he can see himself in them if he's looking. He slaps the door handle and begins to soldier crawl towards the door, thick in forearms and obedience, with war in reach. Everyone is to his or her feet as the last act has come to play. Through the stink, the trouble, and this fertile excess of accomplishment we all will this man out of the door. His determination, however, is simply not enough and as the train doors slowly close the crowd comes to lower their heads as if at the earliest of Monday funerals.

My new friend though, with MacGyver in mind; or simply drunk as the day he was born in Vietnam, shoves his bottle, as an extension of his arm, between the doors causing them to squeal and reopen. What remains of the wine lubricates the steps down to the street. We all give glances for miracles when a train car passes, and on an N train on Second Avenue and Irving Street our antihero has earned his second wind. And pushing madly the sun hits him like the lights inside the labor ward of a hospital not two blocks away. Climbing and crawling outside this train, down corrugated steel steps that cut and warm his belly, through angry loud doors like hangovers, he is born again onto the streets of San Francisco.

Story

I want to tell you a little story about a little girl, but don't you dress it up, in fact: take off your pants, sit down, and try your very best to keep in mind that sometimes the stories just tell themselves.

I was walking down the street one day in a city like a body, everything was fluent, it just seemed to pump, the buses down the street, the beetles that skirmished about your feet. There's a beat that everything takes when it finds its step, like women's menstrual cycles or lover's heartbeats, sometimes it just seems to make sense. Anyway I was walking down this street or an avenue, sometimes you just don't remember the details. But there was this girl, on the curb crying.

She sobbed completely out of beat with the city, like when people are bad at clapping at concerts. It felt sad. She stopped the music in my head, she stopped the movement of my feet, and she stopped me. I took a seat next to her. She didn't bother looking up, she just sobbed, out of place, out of time, out of beat. For the next ten minutes the city life, like a clocks rhythm, was just broken. I was speechless, I only spoke in rhyme; she broke my heart when she broke my timing. So I stuttered, as if I'd stuttered before. The words that find your mouth mind themselves like they were meant for your tongue, like everything you say is worth the air it prattles on. But I stuttered for the first time in my life, like an amnesic patient learning how to trust all over again. I found some words, I think I got somewhere?

"Wh.. What keeps you up, if? If it's gone I'll go get it, you seem to be down."

I wasn't a wordsmith, she wasn't a kite, I'd walked across a few books with my eyes, but the downtrodden intrigued me.

"I just," she stuttered like a bride down a runway, like a model on her May Day.

"I just can't get anything write today."

And I misheard her.

I missed her.

I asked her name in a forgiving tone, I asked her if there were more or less of her I should have known. She would never answer a damn thing after that with a line. Her name was Story. Like a joke I would ask about her ending, if she counted her calendar days like pages and every year, well do your chapters end at the fall of your tears.

Her parents weren't books, her birth was really just an idea they took from the shelf when they had read each other silly one night.

The day of her conception her mother had published a novel titled "Nine Months in Waiting Rooms: *tired heels tied to tile floors tire of you.*"

She read the book as soon as she could read. And she took off as soon as she realized the meaning.

Sometimes the meaning is all it takes and sometimes the meaning takes it all.

But they were real class acts, she would tell me about her parents, "I hate clichés, but my parents would sometimes tell me, sometimes the truth hurts."

She would tell me her little brother's name was Truth.

I would laugh like fiction.

The stories are always best when you read them as you are writing them.

She got it; we would start and stop everything together, like minds at work, like miners in mountains telling stories until we got the gold out.

She got the gold out of me.

And I found her on the curb crying, she told me her name was Story and I started listening, she said the best place to lie like rugs were in libraries where you could never be penalized for not talking enough.

She said she was a loss of words until she found pens and paper, that the best lies like lawyers were contracted across tables.

So we would go to work between our body language and spell out our best interests with the greatest alliteration her mother never read.

She called me the vehicle that all her greatest emotions read, no rode, no ride. We published practically every month it was worth the lives we lived, she said sometimes we would get it right.

It would remind me of that first day on a curb like a child with no parents, she was crying, Story with no story. I told her "sometimes you have the words, sometimes you have the story, sometimes you have both, sometimes, lately, you just don't."

I brought her home and fed her my feeble lines, faulty poems that walked tall in the clouds; they were built on cheap stilts from the diction my mind had designed.

She told me it was all wrong, she, she, I stutter to this day.

She took off her blouse and, like maps in my mind, traced bruises and freckles like paragraphs.

I just wrote like an artist, like a cartographer, like I was drawing.

I found it in her smiles. She lined my life with adjectives and when I was with her I was never at a loss.

How I made a fist until the writing would come, with metaphors, like, nothing else. She would walk her fingers and my eyes down the pages of her life and, every dent in her thigh, every scar that made her break down and cry.

They were her stories.

After kissing her goodnight I would tug at her ear to bookmark our progress.

We were a small collection of dates, a catalogue of calendar days, she would tell me someday if we were lucky, we could be an anthology.

I found with every article of clothing, another beautiful rhyme, her legs were so long I swore my stilts would never reach that high.

We were published, I'll tell you it was both of us, mostly because she was my muse. I was the mouth for all the words she made me think of but just couldn't use.

When I found her on the curb that day and she told me, "I just can't get anything write."

I understood instantly after that first night.

Because she was the story I wrote, she was the violent quiet you hear when you turn the page, of every book.

I'll tell you this right now because you've asked me.

You've asked me impatiently, with the tone reserved after you've asked me a million times.

You asked me with a stutter. You're a pretty girl, and I figured you would know better.

You asked me in a city with a heart that beats and pumps with taxi lights, neon bar signs and lovers that whisper in melodies as they are loving "good night."

You asked me what was wrong, as I sat on a curb in your big city, what was wrong. Like an orphan on a bad night, I thought about love and the way sometimes words just make it, make our bodies maps, make our time pass, in laughs, in sudden cliffhanger chapters I was sitting on this curb crying.

Under my breath, I said, "Since she left."

But all you heard was "I just can't get anything write."

Lesser White

"And it's so cold in here."*

Somewhere in the future or in the past, no, no, currently, just somewhere you've never been, it isn't where or when. You've just never been there, I can tell.   It's so cold they're waiting for global warming, they wear these coats big like everything, so they will never be forgotten and the trouble with everything is there is never any room left for love. It's just so cold. They keep sending me these postcards that say, "Wish You Weren't Here" in the bottom right corner in a rolling Hollywood font, and the postcard is just flat white like the walls in an empty apartment building. I took all these postcards, something like sixteen, and laid them out on the floor. When it's always overcast, it's never day and never night, you'd hate it like the sun is screaming into white pillows and you can never hear it. I've gathered that this overcast haze swallows people but they never disappear. It would be more fitting to say that they are forgotten instantly if left alone, like the outer banks of our hazy memories that need to occasionally be thought of to stay alive.

These postcards they don't have return addresses. They don't even have my address. I actually waited all day for the tenth one with my eye peering outside the peephole on my front door. And as my weak knees gave ever so silently it materialized in a matter of seconds much and most (opportunely) like fog. Here I am one strange postcard a day for the past sixteen days and all these postcards laid out like puzzle pieces have become overwhelming as if I am buried in snow. I am strangled by the thought of never returning these bottled messages to their senders, as well as disturbingly enchanted by this subscription I have incurred, though never wish to write for.

Everyone is a writer when they go to war.

"Can you feel this?"

This one postcard reads like a suicide note though entirely sacrificial and proud. It's written all dodgy like a plane crash love note and the corners are bent in violently. A woman is sending away for a new propeller and seems to pay for it with her sympathies. She tells of an escape she and her lover make from the low hugging fog in an airplane they built for two out of old silverware and dry-wall. I picture a classic bomber leather cap, thick goggles and patched jacket, poorly sewn or perhaps merely riveted together with possibilities of warmth and a loss in the translation of connection.

I am told because of her anemia she can only make love soaring high above the cold white everything, she tells me this like she's going to heaven, like the plane is a real rocket. She tells me this is the only way to go, that nothing else is suitable, that she is in love. Sadly they are the only aviators in the cold white everything and every time they go up, there is a better and better chance they will come crashing down, that the plane is getting old and unreliable. Then she goes on about how every time they go up their love is stronger and stronger, how they can fly above everything, the forgetting fog, the old cold nothing and remove their everything coats. But it was worth it, she tells me, and from time to time I think of a world when we can only make love in the sky on damaged airplanes. I thought about the fear of flying and real rough landings, the commitment to close your eyes and take off without fear. I came to wonder, if when they finally crash, the tears in their eyes will be of joy or sorrow.

By no means do I wish any pain on these individuals, assuming they are individuals and not just characters in lost boys' dreams, I just have no means of corresponding with them. And I would be lying if I told you I didn't look forward to reading them after work, over and over again, like they were sent from loved ones on holiday in Greenland or Alaska, even Hell Norway.

In fact I checked out a documentary on the history of the mail system and found links to deciphering the pyramids, and love letters on epitaphs read by strangers that got lost in cemeteries. This was exciting stuff when you waited tables for the same regulars at the café up the street.

"Don't come near me, don't go missing."*

Another one reads like a medical book, all warm and red. It's flustered and messy from an indecisive man, his heart is in two places and his big coat of everything isn't keeping him warm anymore. Sometimes I have to remind myself my circulation and the warmth of my blood is responsible for the warmth of my clothes, and that insulation can keep the cold in as well.

This fellow, last July, writes in his medical journal that he has lost his mother to the cold. She left his father and couldn't keep warm enough on her own. There's a stigma in this place like Eskimos that forget how to kiss: if you wander far enough into the white haze, you'll never be found. Some families are born and stay together for centuries and may very well never leave their homes; the brave ones are tied off on strings of emotions that save them from being alone.

Love, hate, lust or loathe: the stronger the feelings, the longer the rope.

Now this man, this pre-med, only one in his class has cured the white, has figured out the great everything, figured out everything. He says it's in his heart; it's in everyone's hearts that will keep him or her from being swallowed by the white, forgotten by the world. That death and forgetting are one in the same. He knows groups and families, their hearts just throb like light houses through the fog, that they are beautiful beacons. So this indecisive man used his scalpel to pry open his everything coat, cut himself down to nothing and bare all of his emotions. Now, with half his heart in his hand, he has gone searching for his mother with his father tied off on his strong, strong string of hopes. They have become stretched like a human chain, wrapped red like presents left to wander through a great sea of white. And he knows if he stops hoping to find his mother he will forget her forever and his dimming light will lead to the abandonment of his father as well.

These people always sound so sure of themselves, yet they never tell you how long they've been avoiding or tempering the environment they have found themselves in. Nor do they ever mention when it ends or if they have tried as a town to move to a more clear state of mind. After the second postcard I began to wonder about the Juvenile Detention center on the hill, and about a group effort on arts and crafts day. If a group could construct such an effort to creep out that kid that works at the bottom of the hill, if only to have some effect on the outside world.

After the fifth postcard I began to wonder about the abandoned mental asylum in the Presidio. If the "ghosts" had all been writers gone druggies and had a foggy mail system in the works. Which pushed me to pursue the obvious question, "why me?" The fact that I had outstanding late fees for most great dead authors at the neighborhood library became overturned when I rushed them back after the eighth postcard.

"Are you awake?"*

She told me to read this one out loud, like at show and tell. It reads like a classified ad but is still just a postcard. It's written with different colored pencils and some words like lonely and haunted are written in white, in fact they look like scratches from a pen with no ink. These scribbles of hers wear a curiosity strong enough to create and swear by hundreds of fables. It's in a wet grass field where I imagine her lying on her back kicking the fog with her bare feet. It's on a hazy beach where she sings in echoes, she writes that she wanders one hundred pounds light with a white dress like nothing. She twirls like Christmas and in the fog she plays hide and go seek. She tells me steam is the fire you put your hands in. Nobody will ever play with her though, out of fear or reason, their big coats of everything allow little movement. In all honesty, she doesn't need any love. Her heart is big enough to swallow all the fearful white fog in one big huff. The silly thing is, she doesn't know of her serendipity, so she merely goes on running through the blinding sea with wide-open arms readily accepting someone somewhere like her. She is waiting on a chance encounter to bump shoulders in an immeasurably bleak sort of land, covered in an amazing haze of flat white clouds, as if playing Marco Polo in the dead of night, except without voices, merely hot air hopes that burn away the cold, allowing for sight.

It is very important for me to note that she is menacingly beautiful in her follies. So she writes like calling lost dogs, postcards for a love she doesn't need but she sure wants. I'd reply if I had an answer, if I had a return address.

Night terrors will make you sweat in a cold room; you will haul your dirty sheets to the laundromat twice a week and get looks like you're running a brothel.

"I'm afraid of everything."*

At any given time it sounds like a million things it isn't, nothing like a postcard to a stranger and nothing like a whisper before a kiss. There's the dragging scratch, something like god's fingernails down the scaled back of the devil, marking the fear into him. That's what it sounds like when I trap it in an old trunk in my attic. I don't go into the attic anymore. I've been trying to send some samples, he tells me, as if I asked him for the stuff, but it just burns off in the sun when its disjoined from it's ugly heap and then grows back like the tail of a terrible lizard.

At the west end of town the beaten but not forgotten shed where Mr. Mercer lives is always quiet. He stopped coming out when he lined his walkway with test tubes full of the fog then cursed a different word down the necks of them, like yelling into your own throat, they all popped like a string of vocal chord Christmas lights. People stopped raising their voices that day, the quiet rushed in like a fog, and all we had left were our postcards and our whispers. That day Mr. Mercer's throat became a gun instead of a horn and he shot it off and it backfired. He would tell you, if he hadn't lost his voice, if he only had a song to sing, that the fog would dissipate generously.

"You're the good things"*

I was never afraid of heaven until I finished reading all these postcards, the good, kind people that get by alone in their single apartments, they feed their fish and donate to charity. They don't steal or lie, they don't even sin, they wake up, work and sleep. They read the bible in the same fashion we read magazines at the dentist, and this isn't purgatory, they are dead but no one killed them and their funerals were mostly paid off with IRAs. This foggy life like a coma, this is probably what happens to missing people when we switched from milk cartons to milk jugs. They spent their lives so busy wearing all their problems they never had any time for love, or hopes or dreams. And the after-parties of our lives are meant to mirror our best intentions, the whitest bones of our emotions. Now they're dead in the forever billows of heaven wondering where they parked their cars or discussing the weather, partly cloudy with a chance.

Everyone called life a dream until we fell asleep.

I just woke up.

*The following lines are lifted
"And it's so cold in here" and "Are you awake?"- Tim Kasher- There's a coldest day in every year.
"Don't come near me, don't go missing."- Joanna Newsom- Cosmia
"I'm afriad of everything."- Bob Nanna
"You're the good things."- Isaac Brock

The Eleventh Commandment

In the bible, the new bible, what's going on upstairs today, after the fables and prophecies, today there is a new law, the eleventh commandment. I wouldn't be able to just come out and say it because I don't think it applies to you at all. Besides, eleven is such an odd and ugly number. However, thanks to the gray matter of translation, I can explain it. Reason, "he" said, let's give them reason. So reason with me. My name is Edward, I was an angel, I've been in hell for two days now and they want me to tell you my story. Redemption rolls down the cornerstone of guilt and denial, so "he" says, and if I confess I'll be out in no time.

I guess I could start with justification. I remember long warm nights staring into the laundromats at these women. Really any major metropolitan area would do fine. These women, they had something that you couldn't find in all the cotton billowing clouds of heaven. They were frustrated and confused, some nights just folding their jeans weighed so heavy on them they sulked to the floor. Night dreaming, I would roll over on my back and imagine my finger lifting their chin up above and over their petty worries of the world, and they would smile and become angels, then in an instant I would lose all interest in them.

Their smiles alone made them perfect and perfection, perfection was easy and I did perfection all day. Fuck perfection. Night after night of watching these girls break down at corner stores with pregnancy tests or at ATMs with nickels and dimes, night after night and my thoughts, my heart seemed to fall farther and farther towards earth. I didn't understand at the time but I certainly didn't complain. I was closer and closer to imperfection everyday, bewildered jaw heavy. I remember right before I hit the ground somewhere in LA, I tripped; funny thing is angels aren't supposed to trip. I tripped so hard in Heaven I landed in Hollywood.

I know what you're thinking; it's a long way to fall, right? Well let me counter, do you think after a brutal death, after battling cancer, your god is going to ask you to walk down (up) a (long) hallway? After a tedious lifetime of good work and charity you still have to race a million miles into the clouds. Truth is, Heaven is thirty-three feet above the earth, however with perfection comes clarity, in all senses of the word, so no you can't see any of it, because it's too perfect for your adolescent eyes.

Back to the story, if I remember correctly I fell on the corner of Wilshire and Highland and while wiping off my jacket I noticed my wings were gone and that I was bleeding. I had finally reached imperfection. Familiar with the territory, I started down the street to a bar I had been watching but weeks ago. As I entered I noticed an odd aura. It was loud and wet, but not moist, wet in a sense of your mouth, but never felt throughout.

"What will it be, pretty boy?" The bartender mouthed off to me, and I don't even notice. He continues, "Hey you, drink something or get out" followed by a "*fucking Hollywood models.*"

Such a warm greeting that I have been given on this my birthday.

I ordered up some shots of something special and put them down followed by a cigar and a smile from the cocktail dress in the corner. This is it Edward, your chance at the imperfect girl of your dreams. It's interesting, I think it's the liquor but I feel shorter and shorter with every shot. No, not exactly shorter, but I feel closer to the ground.

I approach this broken damsel. She supports herself with her elbows, and below that the stained, sticky counter top keeps her there. Centuries of perfect lines in heaven and all I needed was one. But my throat closes, and my eyes dart everywhere but into her. She still smiles, she smiles and it almost lifts me from the razing of the alcohol. She smiles and laughs a little, all too familiar with the catch and release of the bar.

"I'll get to it, I swear, if you just keep smiling like that I'll think of something to match." I stutter.

"Yeah, I know, that perfect line, right?" she returns laden in sighs, "Listen, my name is Annabelle and you're certainly lost and in for trouble if you stick around here, do you want to go down Wilshire so I can return you to your parents? Aren't they Giorgio and Armani?"

I get it, I look like a half-wit ken doll, and I get it. This is when I learned how far a drunken stupor can get you, and how much faster you can stupor in yellow boxes under black tar wheels. We go over the basics on the way to the designer buildings that bulge under bright lights. She moved here from some small town in Colorado to major in art, only to be belittled by advertisement agencies. One in a thousand, she says, I'm just one in a thousand other helpless girls with big briefcases of canvas and no time to explain the layers of eye catching symbolism.

Warhol had it right, she says, at least in L.A.'s case: "An artist is somebody that produces things that people don't need to have."

I tell her roughly the same story, different words, different town, different elevation, but that I left because everybody was so goddamned arrogant.

"So then," she continues as we step out of the cab, "what brings you to the city of angels?"

I scoff and jump at these words in confusion and false confidence until I see what she's getting at. "I don't know, just seemed like a good place to start over."

"Shall we?"

And so we do, we enter this hip Cosmo-bar, with pillows and blankets white like winter all over. There is a consistent stream of fake snow bubbles falling before our eyes. We get an odd table snowdrift in the corner and just go at it with words, which I'm never short of, but everything I say sounds so close to the truth to me. I know it isn't, and I can swear, though once again it may be the alcohol. It feels like I'm drifting closer and closer to the bottom of my cotton candy chair.

It's been long enough, she's tired and been flirting on those heels all night. Yet, I must point out, I can't help but notice her consistent doubt in the hourglass frame that keeps her soul, also I can't help noticing that she talks as if she's running out of time.

So what do I do, I do what anybody does with an hourglass, I turn her over at a deluxe suite in the Hilton. I turn her over and she calls me god in the bedroom, and it hits a little close to home.

Don't get me wrong I think she's prefect in all that is imperfect, intangibly of course, of course she is. In Heaven I only had these flawlessly perfect bodies, I even started to call them mannequins. So it's really not why I'm with her, besides I'm an angel remember, I'm pure.

The next morning is odd, but for all the wrong reasons. The clouds come in over LA and my five-ten, one fifty pounds of muscle weigh me down in my bed and I struggle to get out. I kick in those tight hotel sheets; those maids know how to tuck the devil in. Curtains be damned as an angel opens his eyes to the rain, this must be that hangover thing I've heard so perfectly impossibly about. From that morning onward every step I take my feet are heavy like Frankenstein's and every hello I give I get another inch out of these knees until noon when I'm dancing in the rain gutters. I've known Scotch-Guarded wings, heaven is one big water park, precipitation is our god and global warming is damned... I know what you're thinking, what about Annabelle? Well she had to run, I guess, so says the notepad on the nightstand, along with her phone number.

I call her, we continue.

I call her.

We continue.

Six months go by.

Six months since we met.

Everything barrels into happiness and rolls off this figuratively flat earth into chaos. Three words are all it takes, three words I mutter under my breath or yell into the ear of Los Angeles.

I love you.

Every six months is actually another girl in another city, but I don't leave them, no, no, wait. I don't just leave them. I promise they were saying it to me almost the whole time, and even when I didn't want it to happen, I said it. Thinking out loud.

I figured out why I was sinking and floating, every kind gesture brought me up an inch closer to heaven and every sin dropped me closer to hell. I figured that out the second day, so I never did anything rash, nothing too good and nothing too bad. It's an odd kind of happy medium human beings live, and I was all too good at it. Until every "I love you" like a vacuum into the sky and back to perfection. Love was perfection, but I didn't love perfection. I loved the chips in the kettle or the way her slip was always showing. Living like a time bomb wasn't all bad, but every time I went up the eventual elevator of paradise I lost sight of whom I loved. So I started over.

And I knew this is where I go to become something I should never be.

Every six months, for four years this charade went on.

Everyone's a farmer of some sort.

Then on my ninth escape to earth after everybody is in bed upstairs I trip back down on gravity but for some reason I keep falling. I fall and fall and fall way past any sure sign of a foundation. Hitting layers of rock and earth all that hurts like chimneys on my way down and by the time I get to hell I'm already tired.

As it turns out every "I love you" means another fifty pounds on my heart and sooner or later I just went through the floor. Weight lifters never knew what they were in for.

I guess they're telling me those three words are permanent and not staying true to them is some kind of painful guilt.

I love you.

They are telling me that if you say those three words and then abandon them you're breaking some new law, some eleventh commandment or something.

The Coat Girl

Then she says, take me, and then she says, give me away.

I got a letter in the mail today. It was odd hearing from you, though I'd say you were the one listening.

You see, two to three years ago or pages ago or anything, I knew this girl. She had this thing where she would wear two to three huge coats, yeah; everybody called her "coat girl," or "scarfy." A lot of scarves too, but that doesn't matter.

The first day I saw you I asked if you were anemic or a burn victim, some kind of explanation for all those clothes, so many clothes. This for some reason induced smiling, though, to my recollection, most of the smiling was done with your eyes. The way a butterfly smiles with its wings. With a giggle you told me you had some kind of fear that you could lose your existence or something; excuse me, a fear of a purely mental existence. Then you thanked me for merely acknowledging you. I assured you I would remember you and that I doubt you could just fade away. It wasn't until a couple months, when you were undressing, that I understood you for the first time.

You said I was the first to see what was below the coats, and when they came off a single tear rolled down your face. Just one. And when I held your naked body in my arms your feeble heart resonated between us. And in every inadvertent lurch you came closer until I feared you would disappear into my chest. By now your fears had expanded and this was an exercise we would perform to remind you, that you were still here.

I remember, you would say the most amazing things to me...

"I fear death is just a trick, when you die, in your brain, your life keeps on going, but you can't break from the end. It's just like a broken record or a recurring dream. Everybody knows but you. The greatest trick isn't even a trick because the probability of its falsehood is easier explained than its truth."

Or.

"What if, one by one, god flipped the switches on all five of our senses, one a day for five days, like a janitor in an empty warehouse? First would be smell."

"I'm way ahead of you on that one," I butt in.

"Shut up, no more smell, the governments would say it's a virus and we would go on, garlic sales would rise and perfume would plummet. The next day would be taste, people would start to worry, and no one eats out, another "virus." Then it would be hearing, the day the world goes silent, in forests trees are falling and it's finally not making a sound. People are yelling and everybody runs out to learn sign language, it's all spelled out on TV. Mass panic in major cities causing the quietest riots ever. Tonight the world is afraid of falling asleep and the sun is followed by shade like it's pulling a curtain around the earth, masking senses. We never wake up the next day for we are all blind. We're all falling out of our beds and not hearing a single scream from our loved ones beside us. We can still talk, but cannot, because nobody can hear it. It isn't really talking at all. The people that haven't killed themselves wake up on the fifth day. Numb as comas. So thats's no hearing, smelling, tasting, seeing, or feeling. They don't know they are moving because they can't feel it; it's like talking and hearing. They don't know if they are killing themselves because they can't feel themselves. The world in a coma, the deer hop through central park, the penguins wait for food at the zoo. The end of our everything, anything, and nothing, five switches to sleep."

"Does this bother you?" I would ask.

"Every day" you smirked in retort.

And I would smile, and so would you.

At this point you were diagnosed with a severe case of social anxiety disorder as well as some other new depression-era disorder. You said you could talk to me because of my kind face, something like reading my innocence. I was glad to have your company, I lacked in muscle what you lacked in mirth, and I was reduced to a shy boy. I remember it was the cutest thing when your teeth would chatter eighteenth century lower case piano key symphonies, and tape up the eyes of mannequins giving them blind faith in what they wore that day. They say your case was growing worse, though your IQ was rising like the tide crashing under your bouts of depression. You would disassemble government codes and sleep in public libraries. I have to say, I admired your eccentricity and that imagination. I would just hold you for days, I got the feeling you really needed it. Or else, you would just disappear.

One day on aisle five of the school library, you were reading a book by Milan Kundera, it was titled, *The Art of the Novel.* It states in so many chapters a novels' elbow, its ear lobes, its heart and of course how we hear its voice. No doubt a novel book, but you always had this problem of looking at the forest of life, and not living in your own leaf. After that last page, that last literal page you read, you heard it all. The library, once a place of silence, now became enflamed in conversations, no, thick in speeches. You looked at me and said you couldn't hear anything but the books, it became the school cafeteria and every book was talking out of turn. Every author in those halls and halls of books spoke up, telling its story and not waiting its turn. You covered your ears and headed outside in a fit of anxiety and shortness of breath. I helped you out until you went running. From what I hear you ran all the way home and burned your books when you got there. That was when they took you away.

And now I have this letter in front of me. It's from you and addressed to me. Ripping it open doesn't change the fact that I will read it; you taught me once that if I wanted to go to the future, to when we were together, to think about it.

To treat the future like oncoming traffic that passed hours ago.

And when it reaches, match it with what you were thinking, and it's almost as if what happened in between never happened at all, it's an abstract idea, but it got me through the longest days of work. I open the letter slowly making sure it still exists without its coat of an envelope. Though blank on the front except at the bottom in twelve point font, centered and underlined it reads:

Everything Is Nothing.

Nothing Is Anything.

Anything is Everything.

I knew what you were getting at, and I found out those abstract writers of the mid-sixties came to the same conclusion towards the end of their sanity, or, careers. You found that there is a fine line between intelligence and insanity. On the back you wrote that you could finally comprehend every aspect of life, a skill only intended for god. That it was just too much and lead to an absolute Idea of existence, one based in the back of your mind, purely mental. That you've thought of everything possible and now you can't break from the end, you feel like a broken record, or a re-running dream. The greatest trick you say, and nobody believes me.

They have taken away my coats.

The second book by my new favorite author

It's my bedtime and after the third night passed, halfway through the second book by my new favorite author, I finally realized what I should have said to that stripper. She asked me what I was doing here and why I didn't bother to support her girls, the girls, on the stage.

"Because this is how we love each other." She said, in defense of her girls.

It all comes to my mind, as I'm about to finish reading this grandiose paragraph about lying to a suicide-attempter. That lying isn't lying if you're saving someones life, because they are about to end every truth that they have ever known. Which to me sounds like a tree crushing a man in the woods, if it kills him does he hear it? Everything feels better, the chapter will end, and I will go to bed, softly. That is, until this terrible spider not more then a millimeter in size, a little prick, comes to hang so delicately about an inch from my eye. This is the kind of spider small enough to keep you from feeling their leg tapping whispers while they explore your body in your sleep. He falls softly to dangle, repelling on that center of gravity of an ass an inch from my eye, and it explodes on my periphery, tickling me like a long hair shooting off the bridge of my nose.

I jump so quickly with new and ambiguous muscles, first swatting at it, then swatting again where it should have landed, with nonetheless the second book by my new favorite author.

Everything is a weapon in war.

The trajectory of his web surpasses my complete lack of any physics classes in college, which leaves me scratching in ignorance at every inch of skin that whispers just a flinch of feathered teeth.

I live below an Irish family, with a stoner botanist's son.

Oh you should see the garden in the backyard, it was promised with the apartment, but it is as much mine as the second book I rented from the library by my new favorite author.

In truth I can only look and wander through it.

This backyard [insert extensive description of wild plants] also houses just as many insects. Spiders, mosquito's, spider-mosquitoes, ants and bees, all evil things west of my window burrow here.

Here I lie reading and on his way down quiet like a conspiracy this little bastard just dreams of the architecture of my glasses, wants to wrap them up and call them home, bore my eyes out like matching master bedrooms.

I jumped from my bed to the floor, where I shake my comforter in large waves only to find these ghosts of unfound spiders so waver in time when you're alone. I pretend this perfect storm has distended my favorite enemy but I know he's in my room and he's practically sleeping with me.

....

I've settled with Virginia or so she's settled with me, she smells of lilacs and her hips wear fingerprints as if they've been smelt then picked. She only turns her head to sneeze, says she's allergic to glitter and what kind of a stripper would be? The black lights in the lap dance stalls make us so perfect and purple and clean, except for the dents and the more then five grade scars that our fingers crash inside of, leaving our fingers fully extended as if to scream.

....

After shaking out the bed I return to his supposed crash sight, that bastard spider, armed with my second favorite book by my new favorite author in one hand, in the other my Whiffleball bat.

This spider, the snake, he is the rain outside my head, how tired and how many times I have begun with only the hope of finishing this chapter or at least, this page.

....

The strip club I visited three nights before was named "America the Beautiful" and every stripper was named after a state, well sort of. No one signed up to be Idaho or Wisconsin, I can't say I can blame them, I have no plans to ever set foot in those states, marketing is just that here. And in San Francisco the transplants come from so far and so wide, to study medicine and language and to strip while doing so.

What I'm saying is they have a Kansas from Kansas and a New York with the right accent. Carolina is split in two most nights, bipolar works, and California wore her blue, blue eyes like the sea, always running, running into the shoulders and the coasts of the bodies of you and me. I was drunk, tired, cold and only had enough money for the taxi ride home, I told her when she asked me what I was doing there.

I said I was trying to keep warm.

I had nothing else to say.

Oh, Virginia.

Oh, how she walked away.

....

I climbed back upon my bed, taking back and walking tall with my Whiffleball bat. I lit up a cigarette like a dictator and let my eyes pace in ownership as if I own this, my reading, my sleeping and my loving ground, my bed. I began again to finish the last paragraph in the chapter I want to finish tonight in the second book by my new favorite author. By the time I've found where I was in the last paragraph of the last page in the chapter I just wanted to finish, my eyes have already darted up twice.

That damn spider.

I have no trust.

....

I asked her what she missed most about Virginia and she said nobody uses the words "lousy" or "enough," enough. She tells me that mosquitoes used to wake her in the night like kisses, that nobody is a deep sleeper in Virginia.

....

I stood upon my bed; it had to come from up here, it had to come to this. I stare up, and crime scene from where he plunged, that bastard spider. It must be here high on this flat ceiling where there is neither a sign of webs nor any corners to exploit, he repelled from a flat wall, which makes no sense at all.

I lay back down and power through the last paragraph, just reading as loud as I can in my mind, all to keep the tiny kicking legs of a propelling spider quiet.

I know what I should have said to Virginia when she asked me what I was doing there.

"Because this is how we love each other."

The lights are still on and I am so tired, it's half an hour past my bedtime and I can't distract myself when I am alone.

Oh Virginia, you've seen ghosts before.

And the men here, they crawl on you when you're half asleep, and the spiders at my home challenge my eyes like tired red lights and burrow in my tight fists, they curl up in my taught toes, waking my feet from the night.

I should have asked her, how she keeps all the spiders away.

And I'll lay in my bed awake as all fright, and she will be off work by four in the morning and she'll hug the bouncer and wonder if there is anything she can wear after work on that walk home that will keep her warm.

Ten Seconds

A tangle's poor use of cords, just as your tongue's poor use of words.

He wrote his epilogue when he was miserable in the morning time, he said he didn't care in what order we read it, as long as the beginning was where they began and when we were done, we were really done. He wrote out ten paragraphs to tell you where he would be in ten seconds.

1.   Was it the boy and girl that couldn't keep from looking into each other's eyes? And for some reason they couldn't get a word in, because it's hard to talk when you're smiling. Attention is kept, and attention is given. Was it desperation or desertion? Was it a relationship? Or, were they merely victims of hours upon hours of coincidence?

7.   Could it have been this mute boy I used to know? He spent his entire life preparing to die by lying in a box for hours on end. He called it practice, as he climbed in, and with but a small Walkman radio, placed the buds inside his ears and tuned into the loudest static, the greatest white noise, and tried with all his might to keep from thinking. His thoughts (he thought) were his life and without the ability to immediately voice them he dwelled on those he lost. A pen and a paper running like a screaming ambulance every time, and we would lose the ones we wanted the most, like passing trains filled with amazing people we needed to know. And so distracted we become when we die, he found out as he lay down with his empty noise and his closed eyes.

4.   Two mouths shut out to the world and open to each other, eyes closed in euphoria or open to the eternities they stare into. In a kiss, cars crash quietly, in a kiss; we smell nothing but each other. In a kiss we think of strictly nothing or strictly everything. In a kiss, the world could end but not, as far as we're concerned, until we're done kissing. And the attention to the burning house you just ran out of or the mother you just lost, can, for maybe just a second, be lost to lips.

2.   Then, there was a mute boy that dreamed of losing his thoughts and a deaf girl that remained entirely alive in her dreams and though they couldn't talk to each other they didn't need to. They had distractions and were too busy smiling to think of dreaming and too busy kissing to bother thinking.

8.   I think I knew this one better, it starts at a traffic light and ends in ten seconds, and it's like those seconds you spend suspended above a swimming pool. You stare down, you don't prepare, you accept. It's between 5th avenue and Grant in any major city, and it has a lot to do with nerves. And when he rushed in so unforgiving it ended his life. That one is too sad, and I'd really rather not go into who was waiting across the street and why some things are worth jumping for.

6.   They do not all have to be about love or death though; I used to know this deaf girl that would keep a diary of all of her dreams, the nightmares too. She said it was just a journal of her subconscious. She would spend the days re-enacting, to the best of her abilities, what she had dreamt the night before. Something about making her dreams come true. I pulled her aside once, right

before she went home to sleep, and asked her with my lips, what she was doing tomorrow, and she told me with a grin, "I wouldn't know, or would I?"

9.   A stranger across the street or an old lover at your doorstep, a smile. Perhaps it is all the happiest words your mouth can't keep up with so it curls in a hopeful resignation of your thoughts. Like a dream, smiling is merely a collection of thoughts that are willing to distract us into a second that talking cannot say and ears will not hear. Kissing and smiling are merely communications transcending actions; something pure without description or definition, without pretense, like a dream or a thought you just cannot get out in time or tune to lips.

3.   So there was a girl! She lived in her dreams yet one day she met a boy that made her smile and since then her dreams haven't been the same. They seem to be merely a collection of the moments she smiled, replayed in her mind when she slept like a slideshow of a family vacation or a line of commercials with the happiest customers. And the boy she met was always with her and true to her dream scheme, she had but to spend the next day with him and the next day.

5.   I think in the end he couldn't stop thinking about her and to practice death as long as she was with him would be useless and he had a word for it, he called it love. She went home that night and dreamt of him, like she had the night before and the night before, except this time she was walking to his house instead of him driving to her. And the next morning on his way to driving to her he saw her across the street, and he saw that she couldn't hear the out of control car headed her way (nor his mute cries to her deaf ears). So in ten seconds he rushed into the intersection, like taking a bullet, or jumping into a pool, he didn't prepare for it, but he accepted it.

10.   Now in his box with his headphones on he doesn't think about much but then again his last thought was so powerful, like a kiss, so full of life, it bounces through his head for eternity, like a dream, like a pinball machine. Now she is lying next to him six feet deep in a large field where people go to dream forever. And she dreams the same dream like it is trapped in the large box with her, but she doesn't mind. She doesn't mind that all she dreams of are the smiling moments, and why would anybody want to remember anything other than that anyways?

Friday Night

Everyone said I could have written that right after they finished reading it.

Just before it is over.

She owns a polygraph machine and I own a metal detector.

The traffic always dies down.

She's after truth and I'm after treasure.

Sometimes I wonder if they are feeding us cat food from rocks glasses in the Tenderloin. When there is talk of snacks and she brings out that bucket, how our mouths water, we will eat it.

Just before the guests arrive she will remove all the hand soap from the bathroom and then ask them if they had washed their hands. This was our little joke. It's so funny when we just stop laughing.

I used to walk by all those porch light sensor lights on cold nights, the ones that save us from criminals and lovers. Where in bay windows protective fathers and

unwittingly optimistic lovers waited for what they feared
most. Here I was merely hugging buildings for warmth
from those bitter biting winds just setting those sensors off
like stage lights. Enter stage left, the fifth house from my
own bus stop home, she ran out like she was gone from the
wind. She ran out and held me, because I wore the same
hooded sweatshirt as her run away.

She pushed off my hood and said, "You're not
you."

"You must be mistaken."

The lights never dimmed.

And we wore it well, a terrible play put on by
ourselves.

She would name all her poor paintings "a frame of
reference." And wear those painful stretched black leotards
when she painted as if mirrors kept her from hearing or
thinking or maybe leggings came back with a vengeance.

I embellished when I told her those strippers up the
block paint a better sunrise on their toenails every
morning, a sight all too familiar. I couldn't tell you what
she looked like. She was an artist, she was a painter, and
she made a mess.

Over dinner she said, "Olive oil burns down too."

And all I heard was "All our love burns down to."

And I said, "What?"

My horoscope that day read "They want a doormat, not a partner, you should be glad you are out of the running."

And I was wrong and she was not wet cement. She was already scoffed and hard, dried and rough, smoking cigarettes and twisting the ankles of those she feared she would love.

The pasta was fresh from Europe; she gets it from the world markets by the ferry building. The plates and silverware were made in China. I began to wonder what was wrong with everything right here.

In Europe there is a world market selling our goods.

The guests arrive exactly at eight, square on time but they still complain about the traffic, weather or parking. You wouldn't need a coat rack or a hallway closet in your life until you met these people. And everyone brings a bottle of wine.

Across the city someone is scratching at his or her new favorite rash like I spread my new favorite lie; I'm getting that promotion in a one-story building.

"Moving up, growing out."

After the guests leave she holds out my coat like a dogs lead, pursing her lips like she's calling a runt. And nobody is safe from falsified affection. A painter, I told my mother. I do not want to die alone, I would tell you the same thing, after enough time has passed.

Tonight I will sleep on a stolen mattress, my hands soft from doing the dishes. Sometimes I'm pretty sure we're just wearing out what is already worn in.

She has a birthmark like a chain of islands just to the left of her right hip. I kissed them last night as we slept on her egg crate down mattress, I kissed them last night pretending I'm kissing a map and tomorrow we land in paradise.

Just before it is over, everyone knows how to pretend.